This book brings comfort to:

Amelia
....

Merry Christmas 2011

Love
Mommy + Daddy

A bedtime lullaby

mike JOLLEY

i'LL
See YOU
iN THE
MORNING...

Illustrated by

MiQUE MORIUCHI

i'll see you
in the morning,
for now it's time
to sleep.

i WILL STay
aND WaTCH
aWHiLe...

...'TIL YOU ARE COUNTING SHEEP.

DON'T BE AFRAID OF DARKNESS.

DON'T BE AFRAID, MY SWEET.

THE NIGHT IS JUST A BLANKET

UNDER WHICH THE EARTH

CAN SLEEP.

aLL CReaTUReS GReaT,
aLL CReaTUReS SMaLL
WiLL Be SLeePiNG SOON.

aLL UNDeR BLaNKeTS
OF THeiR OWN...

...ALL UNDER THE SAME MOON.

SO WHY NOT TRY

TO CLOSE YOUR EYES,

AND GO TO SLEEP, MY LOVE.

HOLD THE LIGHT,

THROUGHOUT THE NIGHT,

OF THE MOON AND

STARS ABOVE.

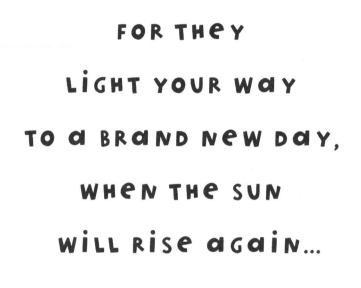

FOR THEY
LIGHT YOUR WAY
TO A BRAND NEW DAY,
WHEN THE SUN
WILL RISE AGAIN...

NOW DREAM YOUR DREAMS
OF SOFT MOONBEAMS.
LET THE NIGHT
BECOME YOUR FRIEND.

THERE ARE NO MONSTERS ANYWHERE.

I'VE SENT THEM ALL BACK HOME,

AND CHASED THE SHADOWS

FROM THE ROOM,

SO WE CAN BE ALONE.

THERE'S NOTHING AT THE WINDOW.
THERE'S NOTHING IN THE HALL.
REMEMBER, IF YOU NEED ME,
YOU ONLY HAVE TO CALL.

ANOTHER DAY IS ON ITS WAY,
BUT NOW IT'S TIME TO SLEEP.
SO CLOSE YOUR EYES,
MY DARLING...

...and FINISH COUNTING SHEEP.

sleep tight
in light...

...and i'll see you
in the morning!

FOR MUM, WITH LOVE, WITH LIGHT - MIKE

FOR DAI & KATE - MIQUE

A Templar Book

First published in the UK in 2005 by Templar Publishing,
an imprint of The Templar Company plc,
Pippbrook Mill, London Road, Dorking, Surrey, RH4 IJE, UK
www.templarco.co.uk

Illustration copyright © 2005 by Mique Moriuchi
Text and design copyright © 2005 by The Templar Company plc

First edition

ISBN 1-84011-938-1

Printed in China

templar publishing